HAPPY! HAPPY! HAPPY!

Author Brenda M. Tillman
Illustrator Laetitia Auguste

Recommended for ages 3 – 10+

BMichelle Speaks
© Tillman, Brenda M.
P.O. Box 366114
Atlanta, GA 30336-6114

http:// bmichellepoet.bigcartel.com
@bmichellepoet
bmichellepoet@gmail.com

Happy! Happy! Happy! Text by Brenda M. Tillman; Illustrated by Laetitia Auguste

Summary: Happiness is a choice, so choose to be happy! It makes life better.

ISBN 978-0-9787751-2-4

1. Children – Self-help; 2. Children's Literature; 3. Children – Self-esteem; 4. Emotions – Happy; 5. Positive Thinking; 6. Self-empowerment.

Printed by Morris Publishing® • 3212 East Highway 30 • Kearney, NE 68847 • 1-800-650-7888

Smile! Being happy is a choice you make!

Be happy!
Brenda Tillman

TO : _____

Author Brenda M. Tillman
Illustrator Laetitia Auguste
Book Design Lin Sun
Atlanta, Georgia USA

III

FROM MS. TILLMAN

Note to my young "Happy" Readers:

I wrote this book with you in mind. You are the hope for the future! I cannot imagine a world without young people. You are special, and so are your classmates, family members and neighbors. You have bright minds and big hearts. You enjoy the simple things in life: learning, reading, smiling, laughing, singing, running, jumping, playing, just *being!*

I am hoping that "Happy! Happy! Happy!" is a tool to help you master happiness. Remember that "Happiness lies within you." This is a simple truth that adults forget. But, if you learn it and learn it well, your adulthood may be more positive and productive.

I challenge you to choose to be HAPPY and read Happy! Happy! Happy! for 30 days. Mark the calendar in the back of the book to keep track. It is my hope that you will choose to have more happy days!

Yes, sad things will happen. Yet try to find the lesson in the moment and move on to be happy and grow from the experience. When I get sad, I allow myself just a little while; a brief period of time to be sad. Why? Because being sad takes away time that I could have experiencing joy and happiness in life. I hope you enjoy reading and living, "Happy! Happy! Happy!

Remember happiness begins within you! Be Happy! Hug your parents and tell them, "Thank you."

Wishing you much happiness, peace, positivity, and success –

In Happiness Always,

"Ms. Tillman"

SPECIAL THANKS

To my youth consultants,

Thank you so much for your input and approval of this project. (Names listed in bold) I trust that you enjoyed being part of the Happy! Happy! Happy! publishing process and reading Happy! Happy! Happy!

Credits to:

Aaron Adesola Aidan Ajoke Alan Alejandro Alexa Alexis Aliyah Alvin **Alyssa Amari** Amber Aminata **Amir Amira Anandi** Angel **Angelina** Ania Anika Anisha **Aneishia** Anna Antonio **Anthony** Aria Ariana Arielle Ashley **Aundre Autumn Ava** Avery **Axel Ayojonile** Aziz **Bailli** Bankole Bayo Billy Bisola Blake **Bobby** Bradley Brandon Brenda Brianna Brooke Bryce **Caden Caleb** Cameron Carlos Carmen Cazembe **Cedric** Chantel Charlika Chavonnia Chidinma Chloe Chris Christina **Clayton** Coenraad Colin Connor Cooper Craig Daniel Daniela Dante Darrell David DeAndre DeAvious Demetrius Destiny **Devin** Devon Diamond Diego Donovan Dylan Ebony Eli Elijah Elizabeth Emmanuel Esan Esmeralda **Esther** Eva Evan Ezekiel Faith Francisco Frank Frederick Friday Gabriel Gabriella Garrett Gavin **Grace** Grant Hakim Halley Hannah Harmony Harrison Heaven **Houston** Hudson Hunter Ian **Imani** Isaac **Isabella Isaiah** Isla Ivori Ivy **Jackson Jada** Jalen Jamal **Janice Jarrete'** Jayden Jaylen **Jazzlyn** Jeanett Jeanette Jeremy Jeren **Jessica** Jesus Jewel Jonah **Jonathan Jon'et** Joi Jordan Jose Joshua Josiah Joy **Juan Julian** Julius Justin Justus **Kai Kaleb Kamaria** Katelyn Keisha Keith **Kelsey** Kelvin Kelwin Kendra Kenisha Kenneth Kevin **Keynan Kira** Kobe Kofi **Krislene Kristen** Kwaku Kyleigh **Laytan** Lee Leon **Leonard Levi** Lexi Liam **Lily** Linda Lindsay **Lisa** Logan Loghan London Londyn Mackenzie Madison **MaKayla Makenna** Malachi Malia Malik **Mallory** Marcus **Mariah** Markisha Mark **Masiah** Mason Maxwell Megan MeKahla Mia Michael Miguel Mika Miracle Monday Monica Monique Myles Myeshia **Nadia** Najeri **Na'le** Nathaniel Navaeh **Neymar Nia Nicky Nikki** Norah North Nova Octavia Olivia Omar **Omari** Omitola Omoladunandi Oprah Oscar Owen Paris Parker **Patricia** Peyton **Phylecia** Precious Preston Priscellia Qiona Quentavius Quentin Quinn **Rachel** Raven Rebecca Ricardo Richard **Riley** Robert Rocco Ronnie Ryleigh Ryan Samimah Sara Sarah **Savannah Scott** Sergio **Shania** Shanice Shayne Shelby Sierra **Shannon Sophia** Spencer Stevie Summer **Sydney** Tanner Tara Tasha **Tatum Taylor** Terrell Tiara **Tiffany Toni** Travis Trinity Tristian Tyler **Tynell** Tyrrell Twanda Ulrick Ulysses Umme Ursula Vashti Veronica Victor Victoria Vincent Wazir **Wendy** Willow Wyatt Wynter **Xavier** Xiah Ya Yarin Yvonne Zabaniyah **Zachary** Zander Zion Zoe

I am HAPPY!

I wake up HAPPY!

On a **bright** sunny

morning

or a gray cloudy day,

I am HAPPY!

I am HAPPY all day!

I eat happy faced-pancakes
on a happy smiley plate.

I do a happy dance when I get
dressed and put on my pants.

11

I have happy face socks
and a happy hat too!

I am so happy I know just what to do!

I'll sing a happy song!

I'll twist and turn and jump for joy!

Won't you sing along?

I am happy 1, I am happy 2,

I am happy just to be.

I am happy 3,

I am happy 4,

I am happy

some more!

I go to worship happy and make people smile.

I am so happy I talk for a while!

On my way to school
or
at home all alone,

I am happy when
Auntie Lisa's
on the phone.

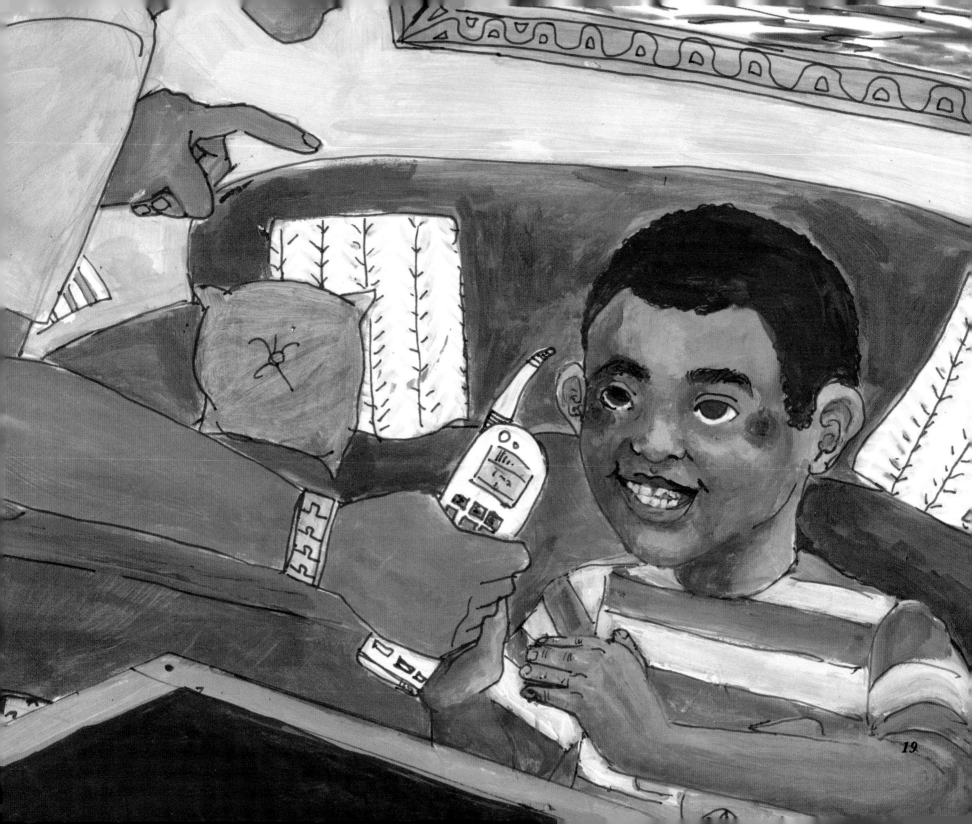

I am so happy,
I will give you a hug.
And spread the happy
feeling of amazing love.

21

I am happy at the park.

I am happy even in the dark.

23

I am happy to sit in my little chair.

I am happy to hug my teddy bear.

25

I am HAPPY with mom!

I am HAPPY
with dad!

And with
mom and dad
I am certainly
glad!

I am happy swinging at the playground.

I am happy meeting friends all around town.

I am happy with toys and I am happy without;

I am so happy I think I will **shout!**

28

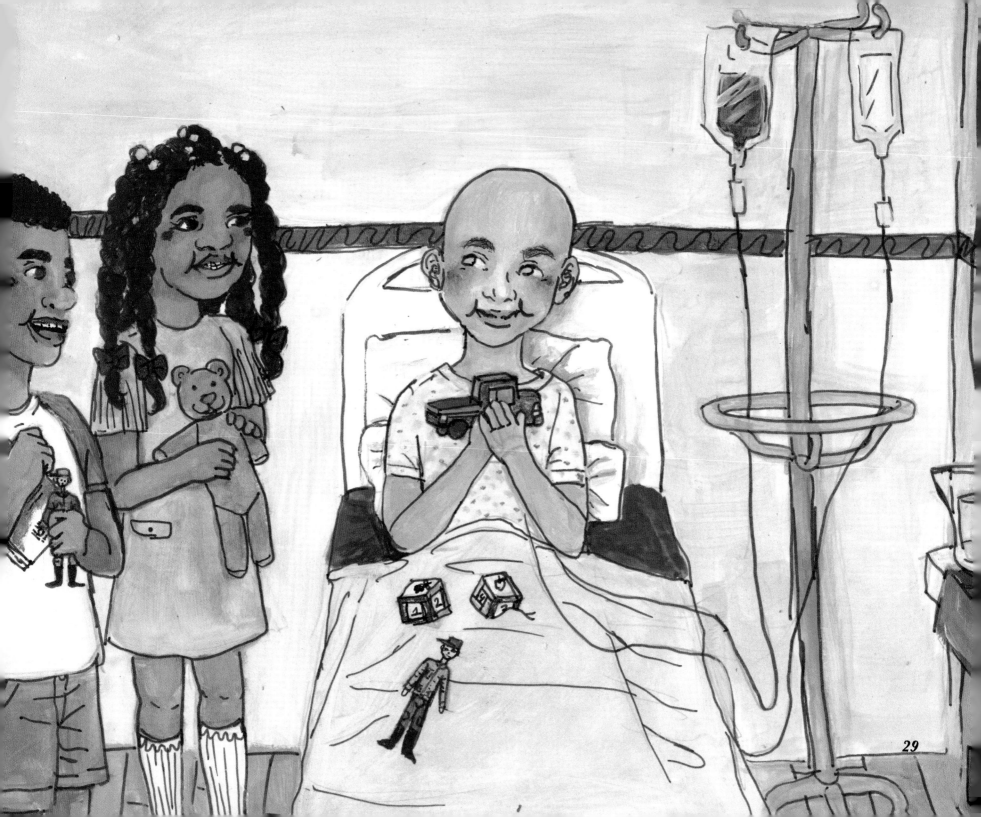

I am happy to go to bed at night,

I am happy there is no reason to fight.

I am happy, so happy, happy to be me!

I am happy, so happy,

as happy can be!

I think you should be happy too!

happy, so happy, happy to be YOU!

33

The Happy End.

Happy Reading Calendar Chart

Sunday	Monday	Tuesday	Wednesday	Thursday	Friday	Saturday

Congratulations to:

Name: _____

Much success and happiness,

Age: _____

Ms. Tillman

about the author

Brenda M. Tillman is an author, poet, freelance writer, inspirational speaker, spoken-word, visual and performing artist. She has convened numerous creative writing and self development workshops. Her intent, when presenting to young audiences, is to increase self-respect and self-esteem utilizing themes of happiness, love, harmony, peace and cultural inclusion. A resident of Atlanta, GA, she was born in Hartford, CT. *Happy, Happy, Happy* is Brenda's first children's book. She hopes to spark lifelong empowerment, inspiration, and a love for reading in her young readers. Her book of affirmations, meditations and inspirational poems, *Listen! Your Positive Inner Voice*, sends a message to all ages that "peace and positive attitudes begin with you." For more information visit http://bmichellepoet.bigcartel.com or email her at bmichellepoet@gmail.com

about the illustrator

Laetitia Auguste is a young 17 year old artist from Douglasville, GA, originally from Haiti. Currently, she is pursuing a career in illustration and art education at the School of the Art Institution of Chicago University. (These illustrations were created when she was a senior in high school.)